Elliot's Fire Truck

Library and Archives Canada Cataloguing in Publication

Beck, Andrea, 1956-
Elliot's fire truck / written and illustrated by Andrea Beck.

ISBN 978-1-55469-143-2

I. Title.
PS8553.E2948E445 2010 jC813'.54 C2009-906830-3

First published in the United States, 2010
Library of Congress Control Number: 2009940775

Summary: Elliot Moose and his friends take a ride on his fire truck and end up being the ones who need rescuing.

Orca Book Publishers is dedicated to preserving the environment and has printed this book on paper certified by the Forest Stewardship Council.

Orca Book Publishers gratefully acknowledges the support for its publishing programs provided by the following agencies: the Government of Canada through the Canada Book Fund and the Canada Council for the Arts, and the Province of British Columbia through the BC Arts Council and the Book Publishing Tax Credit.

Cover and interior artwork created with pencil crayon on paper
Design by Teresa Bubela and Andrea Beck

Orca Book Publishers
PO Box 5626, Stn. B
Victoria, BC Canada
V8R 6S4

Orca Book Publishers
PO Box 468
Custer, WA USA
98240-0468

www.orcabook.com
Printed and bound in Canada
13 12 11 10 • 4 3 2 1

Elliot's Fire Truck

written and illustrated by

Andrea Beck

ORCA BOOK PUBLISHERS

Elliot Moose jumped aboard his bright red fire truck.

"Fire Chief Elliot to the rescue!" he yelled.

He cranked up the siren, strapped on his helmet, and with a mighty push he rolled into the hall.

Today Elliot was a firefighter, and he felt courageous!

Socks was digging through her costume box when Elliot rounded the corner. She tossed him an old raincoat.

"Who are we going to rescue today?" she asked.

"I'm saving *you*," replied Elliot.

"No, you're not," said Socks. "I want to be a firefighter! We can rescue someone else."

Elliot thought for a moment. "Let's rescue Paisley!" he said.

So they dragged the truck upstairs and sped off to find their friend Paisley.

Elliot and Socks spotted Paisley in the library. They skidded to a stop in front of the big desk.

"Look! A four-alarm fire!" shouted Socks.

"We'll save you, Paisley," yelled Elliot.

But before they could unwind the hose, Paisley peeked over the edge of the desk. "Firefighters?" he cried. "Oh boy! Can I be a firefighter too?"

Elliot pushed his helmet back. "Socks and I were going to rescue *you*," he said to Paisley.

But Paisley was already climbing down from the desk. "There's been an explosion at Big Bed!" he cried. "We need to rescue Amy!"

"An explosion at Big Bed?" gasped Socks.

"Let's go," said Elliot.

Paisley hopped onto the truck, and they sped off to find their friend Amy.

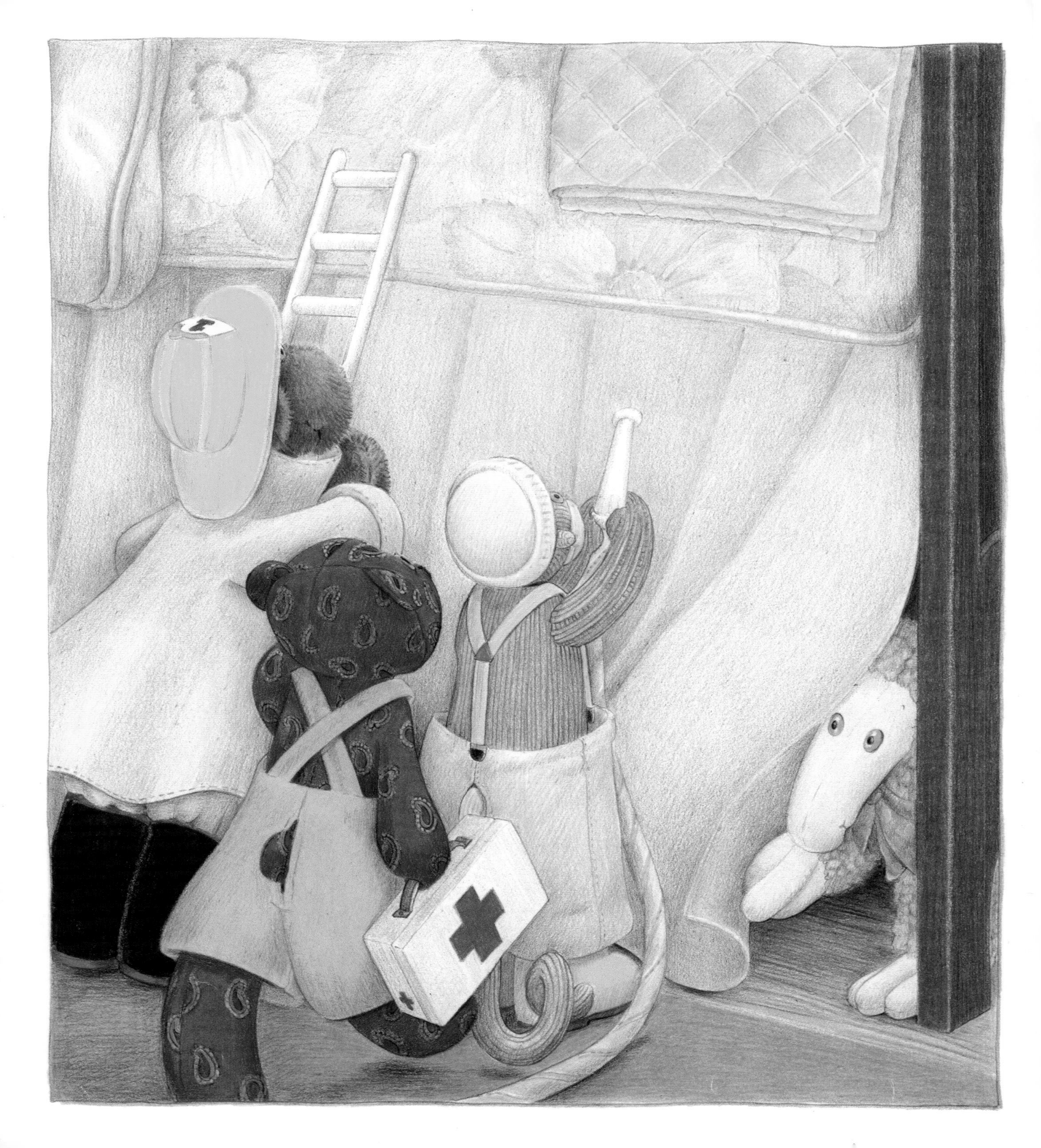

With three firefighters on board, the truck went much faster. At Big Bed they screeched to a halt. Elliot set up the ladder, Socks unwound the hose, and Paisley grabbed the first-aid kit.

"What a terrible explosion!" shouted Paisley.

"Look at those flames!" yelled Socks.

"Don't worry, Amy. We'll get you down," called Elliot.

Amy peeped out from under the bed and grinned.

"Are we being firefighters today?" she asked.

Then she leaped aboard the bright red truck.

Elliot groaned.

"We can't *all* be firefighters," he sighed. "One of us has to be rescued."

Amy smiled sheepishly.

Everyone agreed to rescue the next friend they met—no matter what!

With four firefighters on board, they had to hold on tight. They were about to push off when Snowy and Puff scampered up and asked to be firefighters too.

"We have enough firefighters," Socks told the cubs.

"Besides, you're too little," said Amy gently.

"Wouldn't you like to be rescued?" asked Elliot. "We could get you out of a tree or pull you from a fire."

The cubs hung their heads.

"We want to ride on the truck," said Snowy.

"Yeah," grumbled Puff.

1

Elliot promised to give Snowy and Puff a ride on the truck if they agreed to be rescued first. He felt a little sorry as they trudged off to their den, but then he heard them call, "HELP! FIRE! SAVE US!"

Elliot cranked up the siren. At last, they had a rescue.

With four firefighters pushing the truck, it hurtled down the hall.

"Hurry!" cried Socks. "The cubs sound far away!"

They circled the landing twice and zoomed off.

"Whoo hooo!" yelled Elliot.

The truck careened wildly.

"We're going too fast!" shouted Paisley.

And before Elliot could slow down, they crashed into the banister and flew right between the rails!

Elliot gripped the last rung of the ladder. Socks clutched the fire hose. Paisley and Amy grabbed onto Socks. They dangled in the air.

"HELP!" cried Socks.

"HELP!" cried Paisley.

"Someone save us," squeaked Amy.

Elliot hung on tight.

Elliot looked down. It was a long way to the floor. Who would come to their rescue?

"We'll save you!" cried the cubs.

Elliot swallowed. How could two little cubs help four big firefighters?

Snowy and Puff gathered pillows from all over the house and piled them on the floor beneath their friends.

"Hurry," begged Elliot.

The heap of pillows grew bigger.

"I'm slipping!" cried Socks.

The cubs stretched a blanket over the pillows and held on. "Let go!" they yelled up to Elliot.

Elliot didn't feel courageous anymore. He was afraid to let go, but his paws began to slip and... *whoooa...plop*! He landed in the middle of the blanket.

One by one, Paisley, Amy and Socks dropped safely onto the blanket too.

Everyone gathered around the cubs.

"Thank you," said Elliot.

Snowy and Puff stood up straight.

"See? We weren't too little," said Snowy.

"Yeah! See?" said Puff.

Elliot plunked his helmet on Snowy's head and gave his jacket to Puff. "Hooray for Fire Chief Snowy and Commander Puff," he said with a grin.

Then everyone raced back upstairs to the fire truck.

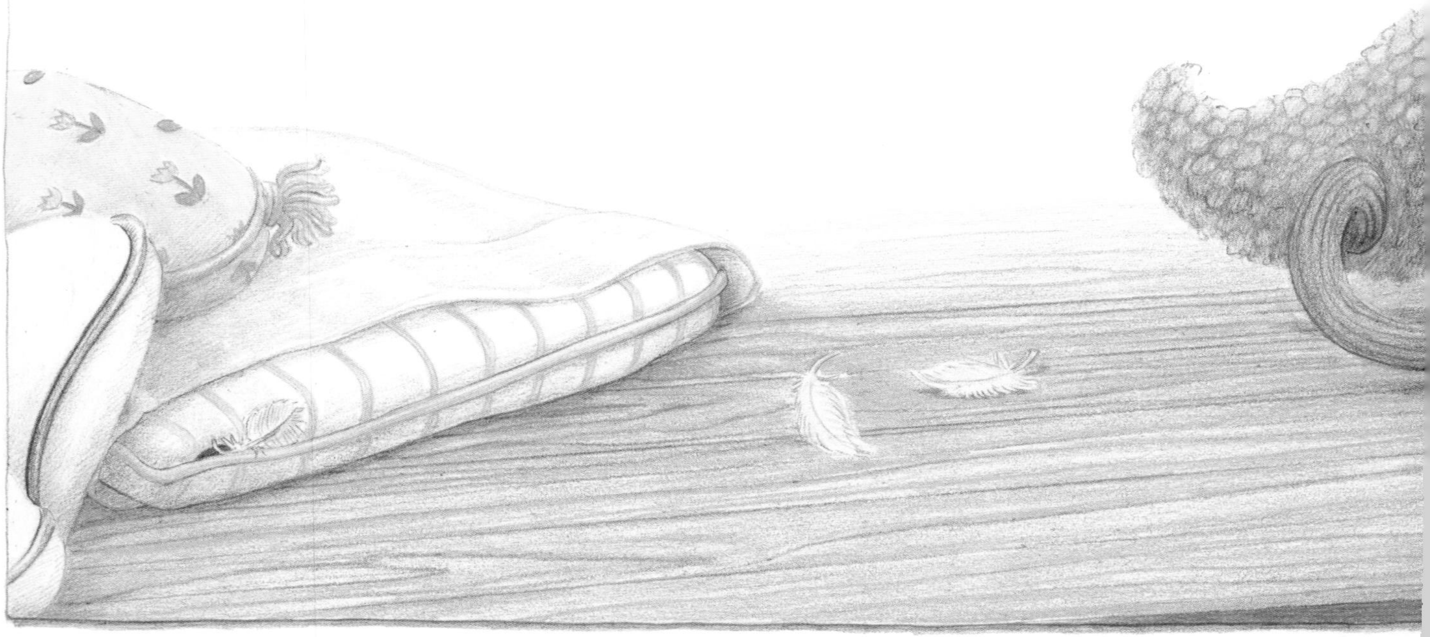

And this time, Elliot was the first to call for help.